THIEF STRIKES!

Hilde Cracks the Case

HAVE YOU READ ALL THE MYSTERIES?

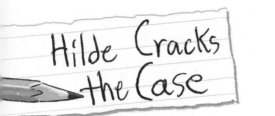

THIEF STRIKES!

BY HILDE LYSIAK
WITH MATTHEW LYSIAK

ILLUSTRATED BY
JOANNE LEW-VRIETHOFF

BRANCHES™
SCHOLASTIC INC.

For the great staff at the Patagonia Montessori Elementary School.
The best school in the world!

Text copyright © 2019 by Hilde Lysiak and Matthew Lysiak
Illustrations copyright © 2019 by Joanne Lew-Vriethoff

Jacket photos ©: spirals: Kavee Pathomboon/Dreamstime; front flap Hilde:
Courtesy of Isabel Rose Lysiak; back flap tape: PixMarket/Shutterstock.

Photos ©: cover spirals: Kavee Pathomboon/Dreamstime; back cover Hilde: Courtesy of Isabel Rose
Lysiak; back cover paper: Frbird/Dreamstime; back cover paperclip: Picsfive/Dreamstime;
88 paperclips: Fosin/Shutterstock; 88 pushpins: Picsfive/Dreamstime; 88 bottom: Courtesy of
Joanne Lew-Vriethoff; 88 background: Leo Lintang/Dreamstime.

Library of Congress Cataloging-in-Publication Data

Names: Lysiak, Hilde, 2006- author. | Lysiak, Matthew, author. | Lew-Vriethoff, Joanne, illustrator. |
Lysiak, Hilde, 2006- Hilde cracks the case ; 6. Title: Thief strikes! / by Hilde Lysiak, with Matthew
Lysiak ; illustrated by Joanne Lew-Vriethoff. Description: First edition. | New York, NY : Branches/
Scholastic Inc., 2019. | Series: Hilde cracks the case! ; 6 | Summary: Hilde and her sister/photographer
Izzy have two cases to investigate for their paper, the *Orange Street News*: someone is stealing
vegetables from the local greenhouse, and a lot of people seem to be getting sick eating the hot
dogs from a local food stand—and soon Hilde starts to believe that the two cases may be related.
Identifiers: LCCN 2018031383 | ISBN 9781338283914 (pbk) | ISBN 9781338283921 (hardcover)
Subjects: LCSH: Reporters and reporting—Juvenile fiction. | Theft—Juvenile fiction. | Frankfurters—
Juvenile fiction. | Food poisoning—Juvenile fiction. | Detective and mystery stories. | CYAC: Mystery
and detective stories. | Reporters and reporting—Fiction. | Stealing--Fiction. | Food poisoning—
Fiction. | GSAFD: Mystery fiction. | LCGFT: Detective and mystery fiction.

Classification: LCC PZ7.1.L97 Th 2019 | DDC 813.6 [Fic] —dc23
LC record available at https://lccn.loc.gov/2018031383

10 9 8 7 6 5 4 3 2 1   19 20 21 22 23

Printed in China 62
First edition, March 2019
Edited by Katie Carella
Book design by Baily Crawford

Table of Contents

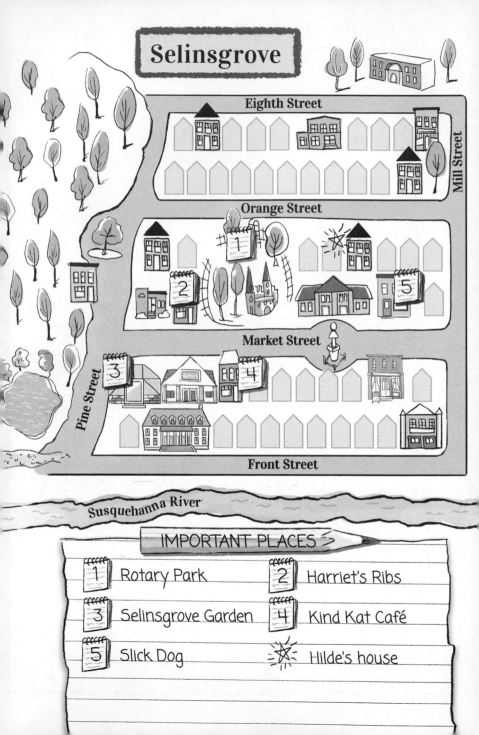

Introduction

Hi! My name is Hilde. (It rhymes with *build-y*!) I may be only nine years old, but I'm a serious reporter.

I learned all about newspapers from my dad. He used to be a reporter in New York City! I loved going with him to the scene of the crime. Each story was a puzzle. To put the pieces together, we had to answer six questions: Who? What? When? Where? Why? How? Then we'd solve the mystery!

I knew right away I wanted to be a reporter. But I also knew that no big newspaper was going to hire a kid. Did I let that stop me? Not a chance! That's why I created a paper for my hometown: the *Orange Street News.*

Now all I needed were stories that would make people want to read my paper. I wasn't going to find those sitting at home! Being a reporter means going out and hunting down the news. And there's no telling where a story will take me . . .

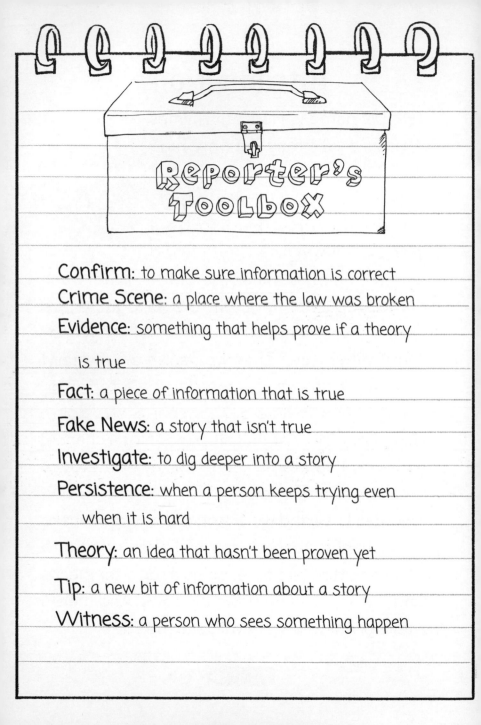

Confirm: to make sure information is correct

Crime Scene: a place where the law was broken

Evidence: something that helps prove if a theory is true

Fact: a piece of information that is true

Fake News: a story that isn't true

Investigate: to dig deeper into a story

Persistence: when a person keeps trying even when it is hard

Theory: an idea that hasn't been proven yet

Tip: a new bit of information about a story

Witness: a person who sees something happen

1 Rocket Ship

The police car's tires squealed as Officer Dee blasted out of Rotary Park like a rocket ship.

"Hurry!" I said to my sister Izzy, "Officer Dee is on his way to catch a thief. We can't lose him!"

I pushed down on my bike pedals with all my strength. Izzy was right at my side.

But our bikes were no match for a car. Especially a police car driven by Officer Dee.

Izzy and I stopped at Mill Street. We looked both ways.

"Which way did Officer Dee go?" asked Izzy.

"I'm not sure," I said.

I checked my phone. It was 2:15 p.m. Our deadline wasn't until 6 p.m., so we had plenty of time to get the scoop on this story.

Just then, a text popped up on my screen. It was a tip! I often receive information from people when there is breaking news. This tip was from Harriet, the owner of Harriet's Ribs on Market Street.

Plants stolen from Selinsgrove Garden. That's all I know, but Glenn has more info.

Thank you. The ORANGE STREET NEWS is on the case!

Izzy and I had just eaten at Harriet's Ribs last week, after we helped Harriet discover that raccoons had been tipping over her garbage cans. Harriet had set up a security camera to catch them in the act.

She gave us a large plate of barbecue ribs as thanks for our help. I told her the only thing that would taste better would be if she put macaroni and cheese on top of the ribs. She laughed so hard her belly shook.

Izzy saw the text and said, "Hmm. Selinsgrove Garden is where the local restaurant owners grow their fruits and vegetables. Why would anyone want to steal plants?"

"I don't know," I said. I looked back down at the text. "But it sounds like we should go talk to Glenn."

6

Glenn owns my favorite restaurant — the Kind Kat Café. He has three cats, and he is also our friend.

"Yes," agreed Izzy. "Let's follow up on this tip."

"Then we'll head to Selinsgrove Garden afterward — since that's where Officer Dee was probably headed," I added as Izzy and I pedaled to the Kind Kat Café.

2 A Sickly Scoop

When Izzy and I walked into the Kind Kat Café, we couldn't believe how many people were inside. The line of customers stretched all the way to the door!

I spotted Glenn hustling behind the counter. He looked up. "Hey, Scoop!" he said.

Scoop was Glenn's nickname for me.

"I'm guessing you have some questions about the plant thief, but I'm afraid I just don't have time to talk. As you can see, my café is *packed* for lunch today," he said.

"Your café is usually busy, but this is crazy, Glenn!" Izzy said. "Are you giving food away for free or something?"

Glenn laughed. "No. Apparently, Bobby ran out of his special ketchup this morning, so I guess everyone decided to come here for lunch instead. My café has been full all afternoon!"

Bobby was the owner of Slick Dog, the place where everyone in Selinsgrove went for hot dogs.

"Bobby ran out of his famous ketchup?" asked Izzy.

The truth was Bobby's hot dogs were just okay. His ketchup was the *real* reason people ate there. It was out of this world! Bobby made it himself using a special kind of tomato he grew at Selinsgrove Garden.

I grabbed my notepad out of my bag.

"I know you're busy, but could you tell us what you know? Did you call Officer Dee? How did you find out a thief struck the garden?" I asked.

Glenn stepped out from behind the counter holding a plate with a slice of pie in each hand.

"Well," he said, "I went to Selinsgrove Garden around two p.m. to pick some mint for my tea. I noticed the door was already open. I walked inside and that's when I saw that Bobby's tomato plants were missing. The greenhouse was a mess of dirt and overturned pots, so I called Officer Dee right away."

I wrote everything down.

WHAT: Missing tomatoes

WHEN: Glenn went to Selinsgrove Garden around 2 p.m. to pick mint.

"Bobby's tomatoes were stolen?" Izzy asked. "So not only is he out of his special ketchup, but now he won't be able to make any more."

"Do you know why anyone would want to steal Bobby's tomatoes?" I asked.

Glenn shrugged. "I don't know, but I can tell you Bobby isn't very nice to his customers. So maybe one of them is trying to get back at him."

"What do you mean?" I asked.

Glenn's smile vanished. "Well, two days ago, I ate one of his hot dogs and I felt sick afterward. I called Slick Dog to let Bobby know. But he wouldn't listen. He even started arguing with me! What kind of customer service is that?"

"Not very good at all," I agreed.

"Now I really need to get back to work," Glenn said. He rushed away.

CLUE:
* Glenn felt sick after eating a Slick Dog two days ago.

Izzy turned to me. "Ready to go to Selinsgrove Garden to check out the crime scene?"

"Almost," I said. "First, I think we should pay a visit to Slick Dog. I'd like to ask Bobby about his stolen tomatoes."

Monday - Saturday
12-3
5-8

SLICK DOG

OUT
OF
KETCHUP

3 Playing Ketchup

We parked our bikes out front of Slick Dog.

"Look," said Izzy. She pointed at a sign in the window.

"Seems like Glenn was right: Bobby *is* out of ketchup," I said.

We walked inside and saw Bobby talking to one of his workers.

Izzy and I knew the girl behind the counter, but we had never spoken to her before. Her name was Courtney and she went to Selinsgrove High School.

Bobby and Courtney didn't notice us right away. Bobby sounded upset.

"Not one single customer ate lunch here today," he said. "I know it's because I ran out of my special ketchup. It is just so strange because when I closed up last night, I thought we had lots of ketchup left. But when I opened the restaurant this morning, it was all used up."

"That *does* sound strange," Courtney said, not looking up. She was busy wiping the counter.

Bobby kept talking. "If I'm out of my famous ketchup much longer, we could go out of business. I better go pick my special tomatoes and make more ketchup right away," he continued.

"You won't have much luck," Izzy blurted out.
Bobby turned around.

"Oh. Hi!" he said. "I didn't see you two there."
I pulled out my notepad.

"Sorry to tell you this, Bobby," I began, "but a plant thief struck Selinsgrove Garden and swiped your tomato plants."

Bobby's eyes narrowed. "My special tomatoes were *stolen*?" he said. "That is not possible!"

"Yes. Izzy and I are investigating," I said. "Could we ask you a few questions?"

Bobby ignored the question. He began walking to the door. But a good reporter knows that persistence is often the key to getting the scoop. I politely stepped in front of him.

"One more question. Glenn told us he felt sick after eating one of your hot dogs the other day. Has anyone else reported feeling sick?" I asked.

Bobby rolled his eyes. "Ugh! Glenn is so annoying! I cannot be worried about some stomach flu going around. Even *I* had a bellyache yesterday," he muttered. "Now I need to find out what happened to my tomatoes!"

Bobby sidestepped me and bolted out the door.

I made a note.

CLUE:
* Bobby and Glenn had upset stomachs. Flu?

Courtney had stopped wiping the counter and was looking at us. Her mouth was open as if she wanted to say something, but then the phone rang.

"It's always a great day for a Slick Dog! Would you like to place an order?" she answered, smiling.

A second later, her smile vanished.

She pulled out a pen and paper.

"You ate here yesterday?" she said into the phone.

I looked at Izzy. "Courtney seems busy," she said. "We should come back later to talk to her."

"Good idea," I answered. "Let's head to the crime scene."

4 All Gummed Up

Izzy and I leaned our bikes against a gate out front of Selinsgrove Garden.

"Hey, look!" said Izzy. "Someone knocked over that flowerpot by the door."

"Maybe the thief toppled it over on the way out," I guessed.

Izzy knelt down and took some pics.

MEEOW!

I looked up. Ollie, one of Glenn's cats, was sitting on the greenhouse roof. She usually hangs around the Kind Kat Café, and I wondered if Glenn knew she was here.

Then we stepped inside.

Bobby was kneeling beside his empty tomato pots. Officer Dee was standing over him, asking him questions.

I turned to Izzy. "Glenn was right. Bobby's tomatoes were stolen, and there is a big mess in here."

"The plant thief swiped his tomato plants but left the pots behind," Izzy added.

Bobby and Officer Dee stepped aside to talk. Izzy snapped some pictures of the pots.

The sound of Izzy's camera got Bobby's attention. He looked at us. But then he stormed straight past us without saying a word.

The greenhouse door slammed shut behind him.

"You should've asked him more questions," said Izzy.

"Did you see the look on his face?" I said.

"Good point," she answered.

I walked over to Officer Dee.

"Hi, Officer Dee," I began. "I was wondering if —"

"All I can tell you is that I came straight here at around two p.m. after I got the call from Glenn, and I saw that Bobby's tomato plants were missing," he interrupted. "But this is a crime scene and I am still investigating, so I'm sorry but I'm going to have to ask you to step outside."

I lowered my notepad. "I understand. Thank you," I said.

Izzy and I walked toward the door.

"This mystery has me super confused," Izzy whispered.

"Me too," I answered. "I can understand someone stealing peanut–butter–ripple ice cream or cupcakes, but who in the world would want to steal *tomatoes*?"

"Ahem!" said Officer Dee, loudly clearing his throat. He had one hand on his hip and the other one pointed at the door.

Izzy and I hurried outside. I checked the time: 3:05 p.m.

Then Izzy froze. "Whoa," she said. "Look over there!"

5 A Friendly Thief?

The line at the Kind Kat Café had grown longer since we had stopped by an hour earlier. Now it stretched outside of the café and down onto the sidewalk!

I looked at my notes and back at the line. Then I turned slowly toward Izzy. I knew she wasn't going to like what I was about to say.

"You know, Glenn's business has been booming since Slick Dog ran out of its special ketchup," I said. "And it looks like Glenn is staying open to keep serving lunch late to make the most of the extra business . . ."

Izzy raised her eyebrows. "Are you saying you think Glenn could be the thief who stole Bobby's tomatoes? Do you really believe that?"

"I don't know," I said. "But you must admit, it is suspicious. Just look at that line!"

Izzy shook her head. "Hilde, we *know* Glenn. He isn't a thief. Besides, Glenn called in the crime. Why would he call the police if HE was the criminal?"

Izzy was right. That would be strange. But nothing about this story was making a lot of sense — yet.

"I hope you are right about Glenn," I said. "But remember: A good reporter always follows the facts, wherever they may take her."

Izzy nodded. "So where to next?" she asked.

"We need to try to talk to Glenn again," I replied.

"He's probably even busier now than he was earlier," said Izzy.

"You're right," I said, "but the truth can't wait."

6   An Unkind Clue

Izzy and I squeezed through the crowd to get inside the Kind Kat Café. Izzy held up her camera and I made sure my press pass was showing so no one thought we were cutting the line.

Finally we
made it inside.
Glenn was running
back toward the
kitchen holding
slips of paper.

"Glenn!" I
called out.

"Hi again,
Scoop!" he

answered. "Is either one of you looking for a job?
I could use all the help I can get right now!"

He handed the cook the papers, then turned
back to us.

I smiled. "We would love to help you, Glenn,
but we are actually working OUR job right now.
We're still covering the plant thief story."

Glenn looked down at my press pass. "Oh, of
course, but I already told you everything I know,"
he said. "I can tell you girls have been working
hard. Can I offer you an orange juice on your way
out the door?"

I glanced down at my notes, then looked back up.

"No, thank you," I said. "But is there any chance I could have a cup of your delicious mint tea?"

Glenn shook his head slowly. "Sorry, I don't have any more mint to make the tea," he said.

I forced a smile. "Got it. Thanks, Glenn."

"Oh," I added, "we saw Ollie earlier at the greenhouse."

"I was wondering where that cat had run off to! Thanks!" he said, then disappeared into the kitchen.

I made a note in my pad.

CLUE:
* Glenn is out of mint.

"Since when do you drink mint tea?" asked Izzy.

"I don't," I said. "But Glenn told us his reason for being at Selinsgrove Garden earlier was to pick fresh mint for his tea. Remember?"

Izzy gasped. "And he doesn't have any mint! Why would he lie about picking mint? He *must* be the thief!"

"It is suspicious, but it isn't proof," I said. "There are so many people here that maybe he just ran out again."

"Maybe," Izzy agreed.

I checked my phone. It was already 3:30 p.m. We had two and a half hours until our deadline!

We turned to leave the café when Mr. Macintosh waved us over. He was our neighbor, and he was sitting by himself.

"Mr. Macintosh looks like he really wants to talk to us," I said to Izzy. "I bet it's important!"
We rushed over to his table.

7   **Sick Dogs**

Izzy and I plopped down at Mr. Macintosh's table. He looked worried.

"Hi, girls," he said. "I'm so glad I ran into you."

"Why? What's up?" asked Izzy.

"It's Mrs. Taggert," he replied. "She got sick after we ate at Slick Dog yesterday."

My ears perked up. "Please tell us what happened," I said.

"Well," he replied, "I bought a bag of chips and a milk shake. Mrs. Taggert got a Slick Dog with ketchup. By the last bite, her stomach felt bad. She threw up three times after we got home. I called Bobby to let him know, but he just blamed it on a stomach flu."

I wrote everything down.

"I'm sorry to hear that, but thanks for the tip. We'll investigate!" I said. "And I hope Mrs. Taggert feels better soon."

"She will after I bring her a cup of Glenn's mint tea. The mint should help calm her upset stomach," Mr. Macintosh said. He was holding a to-go cup.

"Glenn told us he was out of mint tea," I said.

"I was lucky. This was his last cup," Mr. Macintosh explained. "He said he has sold more mint tea over the past two days than he usually does in an entire month."

Mr. Macintosh stood up. "Now I have to run this tea to Mrs. Taggert before it gets cold."

He hurried out of the café.

Izzy smiled. "So Glenn DID have mint today," she whispered to me. "He can't be the thief!"

"We still can't rule out Glenn as a suspect," I whispered back. "He is benefiting quite a lot from Bobby's bad business."

We squeezed our way back outside.

"Now we know there are at least two people who got sick after eating Bobby's hot dogs — Glenn and Mrs. Taggert," I said.

"So should we go back to Slick Dog?" Izzy asked.

"Yes, but it's more like *SICK* Dog!" I replied.

Izzy began to laugh, but her laugh sputtered into a cough.

"What's wrong?" I asked.

She gulped. "Mean-agers!"

The Mean-agers are three Selinsgrove teenagers with rotten attitudes. I squinted. Maddy, Donnie, and Leon were coming our way!

8 Blah!

The Mean-agers were all chomping away on Slick Dogs. Then Maddy saw us.

She nudged Donnie and Leon. "Look, guys, it's our favorite little baby reporters," Maddy sneered.

They looked up from their hot dogs.

"Yeah, let me guess what tomorrow's big headline will be. 'Pint-Size Reporters Learn to Use Potty for the First Time!'" said Donnie. He laughed, but weakly. His face looked greenish. Beads of sweat dripped down his forehead.

I whispered to Izzy, "Should we warn them about those hot dogs?"

"Go ahead, but I think it's too late," she whispered back.

I stepped forward. "Actually, Donnie, that headline is way too long. Headlines need to be direct, like this: 'Mean-agers Fall Ill After Eating Slick Dogs.'"

"We're not —" Donnie didn't finish his sentence. He hunched over, holding his stomach. "I don't feel so well."

Then Maddy and Leon both grabbed their stomachs, too.

"Ugh," moaned Maddy. "I need to go home."

"Me too," added Leon.

The Mean-agers ran off.

I checked the time. It was almost 4 p.m. We had just two hours to get our story in before our 6 p.m. deadline.

I made a note in my pad.

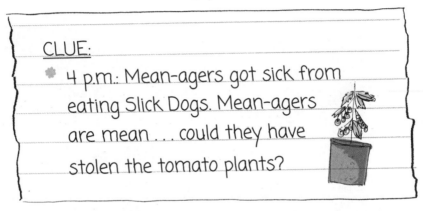

CLUE:
* 4 p.m.: Mean-agers got sick from eating Slick Dogs. Mean-agers are mean... could they have stolen the tomato plants?

Izzy looked at me. "I can't believe Bobby is *still* selling his Slick Dogs!" she said. "We know Glenn told Bobby that he felt sick after eating one, and Mr. Macintosh called Bobby, too. Is it possible that no other customers have complained?"

"We need to get to Slick Dog right away to find out," I said.

Izzy nodded. "Yes, we'll make sure Bobby knows about the Mean-agers. Then hopefully he'll do the right thing and stop selling his hot dogs."

We biked down Market Street and pulled up to Slick Dog.

I turned to set my bike against the outside of the building when —

"*EEK!*" Izzy screamed.

9 Pinky Swear!

Large rats skittered across the sidewalk on the side of the restaurant. They were coming straight toward me!

I tried to jump out of the way but tumbled over my bike instead.

"Did you have a nice trip?" Izzy asked, smiling, as she helped me up.

"Very funny. Could you grab a picture of those rats before they disappear down the street?" I answered.

Izzy snapped a picture. *Click! Click!* Then she became quiet. I followed her gaze.

"I think the rats came out of that window," she said, taking a picture of a broken window in the basement of The Slick Dog.

"Good eye," I replied. "We'll have to tell Bobby."

I made a note.

CLUE:
* 4:07 p.m.: Rats come out of broken window below Slick Dog.

Then Izzy and I walked inside.

The restaurant was empty. Courtney was behind the counter.

"Hi, Courtney," I said. "I was hoping to ask you a few questions."

Courtney frowned. "Bobby said I'm not allowed to talk to you two. He told me that if you write a story about our restaurant, we might have to close our business. And I really need this job."

Izzy and I looked at each other. It never feels good when our news stories hurt other people.

"We don't want to shut down Bobby's business. We're trying to discover who stole Bobby's tomatoes. But during our investigation we have also learned that people have gotten sick after eating here, so now part of our job is to find out why. We want to make sure no one else gets sick," said Izzy.

I looked Courtney in the eye. "As reporters, it is our job to uncover the facts and get the truth to the people," I explained. "And it is ALWAYS right to report the truth."

Courtney took a deep breath. "Well," she began, "I don't want more people to get sick, either . . ." She looked around nervously, then whispered, "I do have some information. But if anyone asks, you have to pinky swear you didn't hear anything from me!"

I reached my hooked pinky toward Courtney's. We latched.

10 Exclusive Interview

I could tell that Courtney was nervous. Her pinky felt sweaty.

I pulled out my notepad.

"What I really need to know is if there have been any complaints from people who got sick after eating Slick Dogs," I asked.

"Yes," Courtney replied. "I've received calls from several customers who have gotten sick. I told Bobby, but he won't listen. Fortunately, no one else has really eaten here since Bobby ran out of his special ketchup, except for those three teenagers today."

I wrote everything down word for word.

"But I really don't want to say anything else," she said, looking down at her shoes.

"There's just one more thing," I added. "Did you know that a window under the restaurant is broken? When did it break?"

Courtney nodded. "Yeah, Bobby mentioned that some kids broke it with a baseball a few days ago."

I closed my notepad. "Thank you," I said.

I turned to Izzy. I must have looked excited because she said, "Let me guess. You think now might be a good time to review our notes?"

"Exactly," I answered. Then I looked at the menu. "Hungry for a Slick Dog?"

Izzy gave me a stink eye.

"Joking! We definitely won't order hot dogs," I said.

Izzy paid for two bags of barbecue chips and two orange sodas. Then we walked to a booth in the corner.

I opened my bag of chips — and my notepad.

WHEN?

* Glenn found the emptied pots around 2 p.m. today, so the plants were stolen sometime before then.

* People got sick two days ago, yesterday, and today.

WHAT?

* Bobby's tomato plants were stolen from inside the greenhouse.

* Slick Dogs are making people sick.

WHERE?

* Selinsgrove Garden

* Slick Dog restaurant

Broken window in the basement

WHY?

* Why would someone steal tomatoes?

  → To eat them?

Could this be connected to the stolen tomatoes??

* Why are Slick Dogs making people sick?

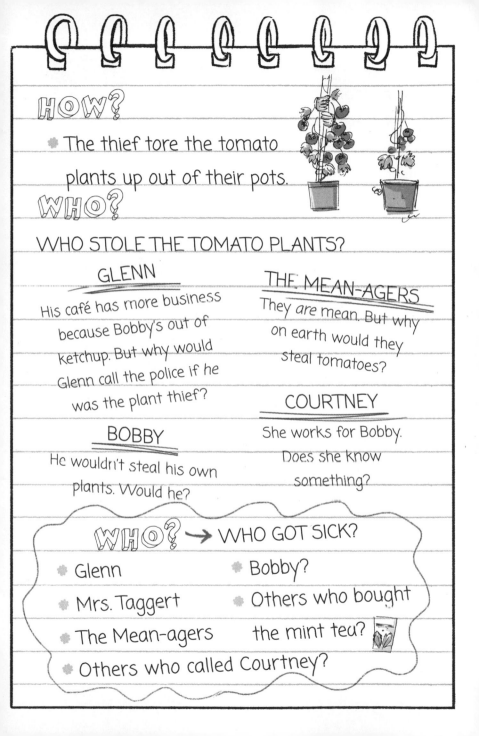

HOW?

❋ The thief tore the tomato plants up out of their pots.

WHO?

WHO STOLE THE TOMATO PLANTS?

GLENN

His café has more business because Bobby's out of ketchup. But why would Glenn call the police if he was the plant thief?

THE MEAN-AGERS

They *are* mean. But why on earth would they steal tomatoes?

COURTNEY

She works for Bobby. Does she know something?

BOBBY

He wouldn't steal his own plants. Would he?

WHO? → WHO GOT SICK?

❋ Glenn

❋ Bobby?

❋ Mrs. Taggert

❋ Others who bought

❋ The Mean-agers

the mint tea?

❋ Others who called Courtney?

I looked up at Courtney. She was standing at the counter.

"I have an idea," I told Izzy. "Follow me."

We tossed our trash and walked up to the counter.

"Could we take a quick look in the basement?" I asked Courtney.

Courtney looked nervously out the window again. "I guess so, but only for a few minutes. If Bobby finds out I let you go down there, he might fire me. He never even lets *me* go down there."

"Deal," I said.

"I'll keep an eye out for him. The stairs to the basement are right behind here," she said, pointing to a dark hallway.

Izzy and I walked past her, then headed down a narrow set of wooden stairs.

11 Creepy, Rotten Basement

Izzy whispered as we walked downstairs, "Basements give me the creeps. Why do you want to go down here anyway?"

"Because I'm hoping to see my brave older sister face down a scary ghost," I said, smiling.

Izzy rolled her eyes.

We opened a heavy door and entered a small, dark room. It felt cool in the room, and there were stacks of hot dogs on the shelves.

"This must be where Bobby keeps his Slick Dogs," I guessed. "It's like a giant refrigerator."

"But shouldn't it feel colder in here?" Izzy asked.

Izzy was right. The air felt chilly, but not cold enough to need a jacket. It felt warmer than our fridge at home.

"There's the broken window," I said. "Make sure you get a picture from this angle.

Izzy lifted her camera. *Click! Click!*

"Now, there must be a thermostat in here," I said, looking around.

"Found it!" Izzy said, running over to the far wall. "The temperature reads fifty-two degrees!"

Izzy took another picture.

Click!

52°F

"Fifty-two degrees? That seems way too warm for meat!" I said, taking notes.

"Let me research the ideal temperature for meat fridges," Izzy said, taking out her phone and typing quickly.

"Hurry!" I said. "Bobby could be back any minute."

"It says here that if the temperature goes above forty degrees in the refrigerator, the meat will go bad and it could make people sick," Izzy read aloud.

"So that's it!" I said as I closed the door to the refrigerated room. "All of Bobby's hot dog meat is bad, and *that's* what has been making people sick."

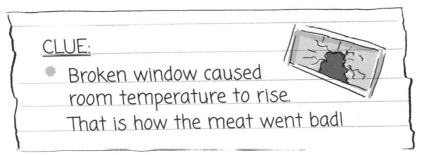

CLUE:
* Broken window caused room temperature to rise. That is how the meat went bad!

My stomach growled as we headed upstairs.

"That bag of chips sure was tiny. I really wish Bobby's hot dogs weren't bad. I could go for one of them right now," I said.

"Hey, what if we stop over at Harriet's Ribs for an early dinner?" Izzy suggested.

"Wait a minute," I said. "That's a *great* idea!"

Izzy scratched her head. "A great idea? You REALLY like ribs, don't you?"

"You're a genius, Izzy!" I shouted. "I know exactly how to find out who stole Bobby's tomatoes!"

12

Fake News Versus Fake Flus

Izzy and I had just stepped into the restaurant when we heard Bobby's voice: "Did I hear you say you know how to find out who stole my tomatoes?"

I stepped forward. "Yes, but what you didn't hear me say was this: We know for a fact that your hot dog meat is bad. And it has been making people sick," I said.

Bobby flashed an angry look at Courtney, then turned back toward me.

His voice blasted out like a trumpet. "You'd better check your sources! My hot dogs are NOT making anyone sick. I won't listen to that kind of talk. How can I be blamed if a stomach flu is going around? You're just spreading fake news!"

He looked down at Izzy and me like we were dirty toilet water. I was so angry, I felt like steam was coming out of my ears. The *Orange Street News* is NOT fake news!

He just kept yelling. "I demand to know right now who stole my tomatoes and is hurting my business!"

I put my hands on my hips. "Fine. If you want to know who stole your tomatoes, follow us."

Bobby told Courtney to keep an eye on the store, then followed Izzy and me outside.

We jumped on our bikes. Bobby followed on foot.

"So, what is your plan exactly?" asked Izzy. "How are you going to uncover the thief's identity over a plate of ribs?"

"You'll see," I whispered to Izzy. "And don't worry, after we discover who the thief is, we'll tell Officer Dee all about Bobby and his bad meat."

Izzy smiled.

Soon we were in front of Harriet's Ribs. We hopped off our bikes. Bobby was still a ways behind us.

I turned around and pointed to Selinsgrove Garden across the street. Then I pointed to the roof of Harriet's Ribs.

Izzy gasped. "The security camera we used to catch Harriet's raccoons!" she exclaimed.

"Yes! And look where it's pointed," I said.

"Straight at the greenhouse," Izzy said. She leapt up in the air. "You think the video footage will show the plant thief!"

"There is only one way to find out," I replied.

I checked the time: 5 p.m. We needed to hurry. We only had one hour left to get our story!

Bobby was talking on his cell phone as he ran up to us. "Listen, Officer Dee," he said, "meet me at Harriet's Ribs and bring your handcuffs. We are about to find out who stole my tomatoes, and I want you to make an arrest right away."

13   Eye in the Sky

The three of us ran inside Harriet's Ribs. Harriet was standing near the door, getting things ready for the dinner rush.

"Hello, girls — uh, and Bobby! What can I help you with?" she asked.

"Hi, Harriet!" I said. "Thank you for the tip about the plant thief. It was very helpful. Is there any chance we can get a look at your security camera footage?"

Harriet scratched her head. "Sure," she said. "I didn't think to check that. Come with me!"

Bobby, Izzy, and I followed Harriet into a back room. The camera equipment was set up there.

A second later, Officer Dee ran into the room. "I'll be taking notes, if that is okay," he said.

Harriet nodded. "What time did the crime happen?" she asked.

I opened my notepad.

"Glenn called Officer Dee around two p.m. today. So the crime happened sometime before that," I said.

Harriet pushed a few buttons. "I'll start the video at two p.m. Then we can scroll backward from there. Just tell me when you see what you're looking for," she said.

The picture went super fast.

Izzy and I concentrated on the small screen. Then I saw something.

"Stop the video!" I yelled.

Harriet pressed PAUSE. We all leaned forward.

Suddenly the screen went dark!

"What happened?" asked Izzy.

"It seems like I've lost power," said Harriet.

I slumped my shoulders. "Talk about bad luck!" I said.

Officer Dee reached down and picked up a loose power cord. "Luck didn't have anything to do with it. Someone unplugged this power cord!"

He plugged it back in. The screen lit up.

"Strange," Harriet said.

Then she pushed PLAY again.

"Looks like we are about to discover who the plant thief is once and for all," I said.

We all moved closer to the screen.

"Watch the greenhouse door," said Izzy. "It's opening!"

14 Caught Red-Handed

The greenhouse door opened, and out ran . . .

"Courtney!" I said. "And look at what is poking out of her tote bag!"

"Bobby's tomato plants!" Officer Dee exclaimed.

Harriet paused the video and zoomed in.

Izzy snapped a close-up picture of the image onscreen. *Click! Click!*

Then I watched as Courtney's foot knocked over the flowerpot outside the doorway.

Bobby's mouth hung open. "But this doesn't make any sense. Courtney works for me. Why would she steal my tomatoes?"

I stepped forward. "I can answer that. Courtney took them because she was trying to protect people from getting food poisoning!"

Bobby's face turned redder than his famous ketchup. "Food poisoning?! There's no proof of that," he argued. He turned to Officer Dee. "You're not going to believe two *children*, are you?"

"You don't have to *believe* us. Believe your own eyes!" I said. "We have proof Bobby is selling bad meat."

Izzy showed everyone the picture of the thermostat in Bobby's basement.

"This is the thermostat inside the refrigerated room where Bobby stores his hot-dog meat," Izzy explained.

"It's fifty-two degrees in there?!" said Harriet. "That's *way* too warm for meat. No wonder people have been getting sick!"

Then Izzy showed everyone the picture of the broken window.

"The cool air has been escaping through this window," I added. "It was broken just a few days ago."

"Fake! Fake! Fake!" blurted Bobby.

Just then, Courtney stepped into the room. "Hilde and Izzy are telling the truth!" she said.

15 Orange Street Ribs

Everyone turned to Courtney. Her eyes were red, as if she had been crying.

"It is all true. Bobby's Slick Dogs have been making people sick," she said. "I told him about the complaints and to stop selling them. But he wouldn't listen to me! His ketchup is the reason people like his hot dogs. So I was hoping that without any ketchup, people would stop eating them — and stop getting sick."

"You will pay for this, Courtney!" Bobby said.

I put my hand on Courtney's shoulder, letting her know she was doing the right thing.

Courtney continued. "So today around eleven thirty a.m., I poured Bobby's ketchup down the drain. Then I stole Bobby's tomatoes. That way, he wouldn't be able to make more ketchup."

"How could you?!" Bobby shouted.

I wrote everything down.

Officer Dee looked at Courtney. "It's good to tell the truth," he said, "but you broke the law when you stole Bobby's tomato plants."

Courtney put her head down. "I know and —"

"Courtney was in a tough situation," Izzy interrupted. "She didn't want anyone else to get sick, but if she talked to anyone Bobby would fire her."

Then Officer Dee looked at Courtney. "It isn't right to steal, even if you believe you are helping people. You should have reported Bobby to the police. Now you must return Bobby's tomato plants and pay him back for the ketchup you poured down the drain."

Courtney nodded.

Bobby pushed everyone aside and pointed a finger at Courtney's face. "You are fired!" he shouted.

"You can't fire me. I quit," Courtney said. She untied her apron and handed it to Bobby. "Maybe the Kind Kat Café needs some help."

"Glenn could use it," I said, nodding.

Bobby sputtered. "Why, I —"

Officer Dee stepped in front of Bobby. "A lot of people got sick because of you. You need to come with me," he said.

Bobby clenched his fists. But then he slumped his shoulders and looked down at his feet. "My business has been struggling. I didn't know why people kept getting sick. I guess I knew the truth but I didn't want to believe it. I kept telling myself there was just a stomach flu going around."

"You can finish your story at the Police Station," Officer Dee said.

They walked out the door. Courtney went with them.

I checked my phone. It was 5:30 p.m. "Izzy, it's almost time to post our story!"

Harriet stepped forward. "Take a table."

The restaurant was filling up for dinner. Izzy and I sat down at a table near Officer Wentworth and his wife, Linda. I typed up the story while Izzy chose the best pictures. We posted the story at 5:48 p.m., with twelve minutes to spare!

My stomach growled. "All this talk about food has made me hungry."

Just then, Harriet walked over and placed two huge plates on our table. They were piled high with ribs. Not just any ribs. Ribs covered in barbecue sauce and topped with macaroni and cheese!

"Check out the new item I put on the menu. I call them Orange Street Ribs — after my two favorite reporters," Harriet said.

Izzy and I clapped. "Thanks!" we both shouted.

I had just stuffed a forkful of cheesy goodness into my mouth when I heard a loud noise.

It was Officer Wentworth's radio: "Get to Grove Farm right away! One of Farmer Jess's life-size zombie decorations has gone missing!"

I grabbed my bag.

"A zombie has gone missing in Selinsgrove?" I said. "Talk about a *terror*-ific story!"

Izzy laughed as she grabbed her camera and we rushed out the door.

PLANT THIEF CAUGHT![1]

BY HILDE KATE LYSIAK

Tomato plants were stolen from Selinsgrove Garden today. Courtney West, 16, confessed to the crime.[2]

The plants belonged to Bobby Clever, the owner of Slick Dog. Courtney, an employee at the restaurant, admitted to police that she stole the tomatoes, but she said she only swiped them from the greenhouse because she wanted to stop people from getting sick. She wanted to keep customers from buying hot dogs that had gone bad.[3]

PHOTO CREDIT: ISABEL ROSE LYSIAK

"Bobby's Slick Dogs have been making people sick," said Courtney. "I poured Bobby's ketchup down the drain. Then I stole Bobby's tomatoes. That way, he wouldn't be able to make more ketchup. I was hoping that without any ketchup, people would stop eating them — and stop getting sick." [4]

The *Orange Street News* investigation discovered that the meat had gone bad due to a broken window in the refrigerated basement. Rats were also spotted coming out of the restaurant. Slick Dog has been shut down until it can be reviewed by the Health Inspector. [5]

Courtney will return the tomato plants and repay Bobby for the ketchup she washed down the drain. [6]

1. HEADLINE 2. LEDE 3. NUT 4. QUOTE 5. SUPPORT 6. KICKER

WHO? Hilde Lysiak

WHAT? Hilde is the real-life publisher of her own newspaper, the *Orange Street News*! You can read her work at orangestreetnews.com.

WHEN? Hilde began her newspaper when she was seven years old with crayons and paper. Today, she has millions of readers!

WHERE? Hilde lives in Selinsgrove, Pennsylvania.

WHY? Hilde loves adventure, is super curious, and believes that you don't have to be a grown-up to do great things in the world!

HOW? Tips from people just like you make Hilde's newspaper possible!

Matthew Lysiak is Hilde's dad and coauthor. He is a former reporter for the *New York Daily News*.

Joanne Lew-Vriethoff was born in Malaysia and grew up in Los Angeles. She received her B.A. in illustration from Art Center College of Design in Pasadena. Today, Joanne lives in Amsterdam, where she spends much of her time illustrating children's books.

Hilde Cracks the Case

THIEF STRIKES!

Questions & Activities

1) Hilde and Izzy think Glenn is a suspect. Why? Reread Chapters 5 and 6 to find **two** reasons.

2) Bobby runs out of his special ketchup. What ingredient does he need to make the ketchup? Why can't he make more?

3) People can get food poisoning if they eat meat that has not been stored at the right temperature. How do Hilde and Izzy confirm Bobby's hot dog meat has gone bad?

4) How does a security camera help Hilde solve the mystery?

5) A simile uses the words "like" or "as" to compare two things. For example, on page 1, "Officer Dee blasted out of Rotary Park like a rocket ship." Write your own simile to describe a fast-moving car.